Wolfgang Steih

The Painter on Floor Thirty-Six

AF210089

Wolfgang Steih

The Painter on Floor Thirty-Six

A Novel

Bibliographic information of the German National Library:
The German National Library lists this publication in the German National Bibliography; detailed bibliographic data is available online at http://dnb.dnb.de.

The automated analysis of this work in order to extract information, particularly regarding patterns, trends, and correlations pursuant to Section 44b of the German Copyright Act (UrhG) ("text and data mining"), is prohibited.

© 2025 Wolfgang Steih

Publisher: BoD · Books on Demand GmbH, Überseering 33, 22297 Hamburg, bod@bod.de

Printing: Libri Plureos GmbH, Friedensallee 273, 22763 Hamburg

ISBN: 978-3-8192-4962-4

Table of Content

I

Dedication

Inspired by *Vincent,*
a song by Don McLean,
written as a tribute to Vincent van Gogh.

Its commonly known opening lyric,
"Starry, Starry Night",
is a reference to Van Gogh's 1889 painting
The Starry Night.
This song was released on
McLean's 1971 American Pie album.

This book is for all those
who refuse to be discouraged by failure,
who continue to paint,
and who bravely chart new paths
through the unknown.

The Incident

I, for my part, paid little attention to the two women who entered the Pavilion Marcour through the west wing. I quickly filed them under *young, art-enthusiastic crowd* — an ever-growing category. With their well-groomed appearance, they blended seamlessly into the circle of guests. Their stylish outfits, typical of Frankfurt's banking district, reflected the polished confidence so common among the younger generation.

And yet, something about them was unsettling. They whispered constantly, shielding their mouths with their hands, as if the mere movement of their lips might betray some forbidden secret. They also kept in motion, always maintaining a deliberate distance from the other guests — a detail that, the longer I watched, grew more conspicuous.

A woman stepped up to the microphone, cleared her throat, and within seconds commanded the full attention of the room. Conversations fell away; all eyes turned toward her.

But just as she opened her mouth to speak, two dull thuds rang out — the sound of something soft but heavy hitting the floor. Like sacks of flour toppling from a supermarket shelf, splitting open on impact, and waiting silently to be discovered.

A ripple of alarm passed through the crowd. Turning, I saw it: one of the large panel paintings had been struck. A neon-colored, gelatinous mass — thick and slow-moving like lava — oozed across the canvas. It met a diagonal river of carmine red; the colors merged briefly before slithering toward the frame, clinging for a moment before surrendering, drop by heavy drop, onto the marble floor below.

The artist — a young woman I recognized from the catalog — rushed forward, sobbing, stunned, teetering on the edge of collapse as she stood before her vandalized work.

The two women — now revealed as climate activists — seized their moment. They scattered flyers across the floor, shouting slogans and urgent demands for action. Before they could glue themselves to the painting's frame, security guards wrestled them away.

Still, their cries echoed through the room: *We are in a climate emergency, and no one is protecting the climate! There will be no art on a dead planet!*

The murmur among the guests swelled. Some reacted with outrage, others with curiosity; a few, though only in whispers, revealed a glimmer of sympathy.

Before long, the defaced painting was covered with plastic sheeting. Cleaning staff swept up the mess and gathered the scattered leaflets. The activists, escorted outside to scattered applause, were gone.

A member of the organizing team took the microphone and offered a few soothing words: "Everything is under control. The situation is under control, and the opening of the Art Fair will proceed shortly."

But doubts gnawed at me: *Can events like these ever truly be controlled? And isn't the very attempt to control them, perhaps, an illusion?*

"Where there is great light,

the shadow is deeper."

— Johann Wolfgang von Goethe

The Ray of Light

Just in time for the opening of the exhibition, the thin veil of clouds parted, and the first rays of spring sunlight found their way into the Renaissance walls of Kranichstein Castle. A stream of golden light poured through the glass windows of the centrally located Pavilion Marcour, perfectly illuminating the exhibition space — as if nature herself had been enlisted to bless the occasion.

The head of cultural sponsorship from the local financial institute took the microphone, his voice steady but brief as he addressed the earlier disruption:
"We understand the concerns of the protesters regarding climate policy," he said. "But we appeal to you not to vent your anger on art. Art bears no blame for the climate catastrophe. It is, in itself, a treasure worth protecting. It is now up to legislation to find the proper answer to this form of protest."

He paused, then continued, his tone warming: "Dear guests, dear artists, dear sponsors — with today's event, we seek to honor an essential idea of our founder, Johann Friedrich Schlingmann, who passed away in 1816. It is easy enough to say that art beautifies daily life, but one must remember: for centuries, painted and printed images were so elaborate to produce that owning one was an unimaginable luxury. Then as now, nothing — absolutely nothing — can replace the experience of calling an original work your own. To hold it, to live with it, to admire it again and again within your own walls."

His words found a receptive audience. You could see it in their faces — as if each person had been reminded of something long known but briefly forgotten.

"And so," he concluded, "I wish you — and all the artists — a successful day at our Art Fair. Soak in the atmosphere of this magnificent pavilion. I am certain you will find a work that speaks to your desires. It should not be difficult, for the quality of the pieces on display this year is truly exceptional."

After thanking the contributors and sponsors for their dedication, he gently dismissed the audience, noting with a smile that his institute fully intended to acquire promising works again this year — just as they had the year before.

The guests needed little encouragement. With a flutter of laughter and champagne flutes raised, they streamed toward the paintings, drawings, and sculptures, chattering excitedly.

The artists — myself among them — were already waiting by our works, palms damp with nerves,

14

cheeks flushed with anticipation. Our stage fright was unmistakable.

I, Anne-Marie Schneidermann — or rather, Charlotte Caprolat, as I signed my work — stood beside my Impressionist paintings.

At last, I had arrived. By participating in this exhibition, I dared to hope that I had finally gained entry into the high society of the art world. The years of deprivation and disappointment, I promised myself, would now be relegated to the past.

No longer would I have to endure the small humiliations —

"Is this your latest prize?"

"Could you do this in 90×125 format?"

"Would you paint this in magenta for my mother-in-law?"

Those careless, wounding questions would no longer haunt my career.

Here, today, everything was meant to change.

*"We are not satisfied
with the manna of recognition;*

*we long for
the poison of flattery."*

— Marie von Ebner-Eschenbach

The Art of Praise

"Madame Caprolat, the range of colors in your paintings is simply breathtaking. Would you share with our readers how you select and mix your colors to create such vibrant compositions?"

The reporter from the local press perched his glasses atop his head, his expression bright with expectation.

"I follow my instincts," I answered with a small smile. "It's a largely intuitive process."

Undeterred, he pressed on, his voice eager: "Your paintings possess a fascinating depth and expressiveness. Could you tell us more about your creative process — the emotions that shape your work?"

I nodded, feeling the familiar mixture of pride and self-consciousness swell in my chest. "I find inspiration everywhere — in my surroundings, in literature, in the work of other artists, or simply in personal experience. During the painting process, I experiment with different elements, often reworking parts of the canvas several times. It's an iterative journey, and it may take many passes before I reach a point where I'm truly satisfied."

He raised a finger, signaling one last question: "The way you capture light and shadow is truly masterful. How do you experiment with lighting effects, and what role do they play in your art?"

But before I could respond, my attention faltered. Across the room, an older couple had paused before my painting *Water Lily Pond*, their heads tilted in contemplation.

I kept my eyes fixed on them, tuning out the reporter's final question, sensing something more important unfolding.

The woman — significantly smaller than her companion — had chosen, despite her generous figure, to wear a tight-fitting dress adorned with thick red polka dots. From a distance, her wide-brimmed hat, tilted precariously, evoked the shape of a Venetian gondola — a flourish that would surely have drawn stares at Ascot. Her swollen feet strained against pumps at least two sizes too small, and her handbag was so compact it could barely accommodate more than a lipstick and a credit card.

The man beside her, by contrast, wore a loose, coarse linen suit that looked as though it had wandered off the set of *Fitzcarraldo*. His once brown-and-white Oxford shoes gleamed with a polish that outshone even the marble floor. It was, I decided, a draw.

They studied the price list, confusion playing openly on their faces. He flipped the leaflet back and forth, growing impatient, and finally dismissed it with a wave.

"No matter what the price is," he said, pushing her gently but insistently toward me, "let's buy it before someone else snatches it away."

He loomed over me, a tall figure bending down with a trusting smile. "Your ticket, please," he said warmly.

I blinked at him, baffled. "Pardon?"

"Your ticket!" he repeated, as though that explained everything.

*"The real voyage of discovery
consists not in seeking
new landscapes,*

but in having new eyes."

— Marcel Proust

Ticket Turbulence

Utterly confused, I found myself staring into the round, poorly shaved face of a man in his late forties. He wore a dark blue uniform embroidered with *RMV Service Team.*

He had tapped me on the shoulder — discreetly, but with firm intent — and now regarded me with expectant impatience.

There was no mistaking it now: I was no longer bathed in the golden light of Kranichstein Castle. I was sitting in the open carriage of subway S5, rumbling toward Frankfurt Central Station.

The inspector had jolted me out of one of my daydreams.

I glanced down at myself, as if the ground beneath my feet had vanished. My gaze zigzagged through the compartment: from windows to benches, across handrails, past emergency signs and transit maps — once, twice — before finally landing back on the ticket inspector's face.

In those brief moments of mental flight, I had been grappling with my innermost longings, fears, and fragile hopes. I knew — painfully — that my fantasies were a retreat, a soft refuge from daily life.

But did they help me sharpen my goals? Or simply blur them further? A familiar wave of doubt crept in, cold and unwelcome.

Around me, the seats were sparsely occupied. Rush hour had long passed. Most passengers scrolled their phones, oblivious to the world beyond the screens.

Through the window, the skyline of Frankfurt's banking district flickered and fractured. Over the loudspeaker, a woman's voice announced: *"Next stop: Frankfurt Fair. Exit to the left in the direction of travel."*

Only then did I notice the second inspector — bulkier, not moving, a human barricade in the aisle. Gripping his imitation-leather belt with both hands, he moved only his head, scanning tickets with the slow authority of someone long accustomed to obedience.

When our eyes met, he frowned. He straightened, tilted his head back, jutted his chin forward — locking me in a stare better suited for cracking the vaults of the European Central Bank.

The scene was taking on a menacing edge.

"Hello, young lady — well? What's going on?" the first inspector snapped, louder now.

Fear and helplessness twisted inside me. "Yes, just a moment — I do have a ticket," I stammered, hastily setting aside the letter I'd been clutching.

Both hands dove into my coat pockets.

Nothing.

My face betrayed everything: the fear, the dread, the hollow panic.

"All art is a kind of confession,
more or less oblique.

All artists,
if they are to survive,
are forced,
at last,
to tell the whole story."

— James Baldwin

Ascent to Floor 36

I found the ticket just in time — wedged between the folded banknotes in my wallet.

Perhaps I could have walked from the Central Station to the *MainTower* in a few minutes. But after all the commotion, I was too shaken to let Google Maps usher me through the city center.

Instead, I sank into the back seat of a taxi and reread — for the hundredth time — the now thoroughly battered letter:

"…We are pleased to inform you that, based on the recommendation of our local agency, you have been identified to participate in this year's Art-Fair at Kranichstein Castle… Kindly attend a meeting at our Frankfurt headquarters in the MainTower, Neue Mainzer Straße 52–58…"

When we arrived, the driver opened the door with a practiced gesture and pointed toward the entrance. Grateful for the generous tip, he smiled and handed me his business card: *Taxi-Murk — 24 hours, 7 days a week.* On the back, neatly written: *Darbandi*, his mobile number.

As I approached the revolving door, it began to spin — drawing me in with a kind of magical timing.

The lobby stood in striking contrast to the Tower's exterior.

Inside, I was greeted by soft, earthy colors and elegant lounge furniture. The expansive space balanced restraint with refinement: pale natural stone walls, Bauhaus pendant lights in perfect symmetry, and marble-patterned floors that gleamed beneath the glow.

A display rack overflowed with brochures. Above it, a screen streamed headlines and stock updates — a world in motion.

I felt as if I'd stepped into another dimension.

A man from a private security firm, doubling as receptionist, greeted me from behind a raised desk. Behind him, a glowing board listed names: banks, insurers, law firms. Power, rendered in Helvetica.

After checking my name and ID, he handed me a keycard. "This will take you directly to Floor 36," he said. "You'll be met there."

His voice was warm, calm. Something in his tone reached me — a small offering of dignity.

It was exactly what I had been missing for so long.

And with it, my confidence stirred — tentative, but rising.

"Art is the lie that enables us

to realize the truth."

— Pablo Picasso

The Elevator to the Lion's Den

The elevator doors slid open, releasing a wash of subtle lounge music. The cabin — glass-walled, sleek — was large enough to carry ten people comfortably.

The digital display above glowed: *Floor 36 – Art-Fair.* The doors closed behind me without a sound.

Alone, I checked my reflection in the mirrored wall. The dress sat well, the lipstick held, the hairstyle obeyed. Everything, I decided, was as it should be.

From the eighth floor upward, the elevator revealed its true purpose: panoramic ascent. Below, the building's wider base faded; above, the glass sheath offered a vertiginous view.

The Wetterau hills rolled into view, the silhouette of the Taunus hills rising beyond. The horizon shimmered with the kind of light that belongs more to memory than reality.

With every floor, my spirits lifted. A soft euphoria crept in — one I'd reserved for the fleeting escapes of my daydreams.

Now, for the first time, it felt real.

I had arrived — not just at Floor 36, but in a world where money, power, and art intertwined. And somehow, impossibly, I belonged.

*

"Please take a seat on this side of the table," said a voice. A woman gestured briefly toward a tea trolley without lifting her eyes from her laptop. "Help yourself to coffee and pastries."

The conference room, like its host, was cool and efficient — minimalism with a price tag.

I poured a coffee and sat, glancing across the table with hope and apprehension.

Opposite me sat a woman in a razor-cut black suit, softened only by a pale pink blouse. Her short blonde hair was styled with corporate precision.

"Ms. — uh — Schneidermann? Or do you prefer Caprolat?"

I smiled, attempting lightness. "Schneidermann is fine. Charlotte Caprolat is just my artist name — for the paintings, you see..."

"Yes, of course," she replied, faintly amused. "We get that a lot."

Then her gaze locked on mine — flat, unblinking.

"I'm on a tight schedule," she said. "We have 45 minutes instead of the planned 60. But that should be enough."

Without waiting, she launched into the agenda: "I suggest we begin with the selected works, then cover the financial terms, and finally the contract. If you have questions, feel free to interrupt."

She didn't blink as she picked up a remote, pointed it toward the ceiling, and activated the projector.

It came to life with a soft hum — obedient, sterile — casting a pale light onto the far wall.

"I always feel the moment before a

disaster is a moment of grace."

— Michael Ondaatje

Thirty-Six Floors Above Doubt

With a small nod, I signaled my agreement and took an awkward sip of coffee. Everything here seemed to follow a predefined script — one I had no role in writing, and even less power to revise.

I held myself back: consciously cautious, almost deferential. After all, this was my first major exhibition, and I wasn't about to jeopardize it with an ill-timed comment or a misjudged remark.

As the projector began casting the first of my paintings onto the screen, my counterpart began to speak: "First of all, space is limited. Second, the bank has set a requirement — each participant must present a minimum of five, maximum of eight works. Based on the CD submitted by your agency, I've made a preliminary selection."

Tension coiled inside me until it became almost unbearable. I had to release it somehow.

Then, without thinking, I blurted out, far too indignant: "What do you mean — *each participant*? I thought I was the only exhibitor."

I had no idea what possessed me to say such a thing. Maybe it was a rush of endorphins.

Maybe I was trying to break the stiffness of the moment with a bold quip.

Whatever the reason — it was the wrong tone, at the worst possible time.

I considered salvaging it with a smile, but I already knew I'd missed my chance. That train had left the station at full speed, and I was still on the platform, watching it vanish into the distance.

Later, I would scold myself. A simple laugh, a lighthearted *"just kidding!"* might have softened the blow, might have saved the moment. It would've been worth a try.

But there, thirty-six floors above the earth, no such words would come to my lips.

A painful silence descended, while my hand was tightening the coffee cup. I felt cold rise from my feet, crawl along my spine, and tighten the muscles in my neck. I had no idea how to re-enter the conversation — or whether I even could.

Across from me, she stared with startled disapproval, as if I'd just asked whether water could be diluted further or if she knew another word for *synonym.*

But of course, she was the professional. And she was the first to recover.

With practiced poise, she folded her hands at the table's edge. Then, after a slight pause, she looked me directly in the eye. She coated my name with a syrupy glaze and said, slowly, clearly, with calculated precision:

"Dear Ms. Schneidermann... the Pavilion Marcour covers approximately 850 square meters. I don't believe you can fill that space on your own — not even if you paint day and night until you pass out."

*"Art enables us to find ourselves
and lose ourselves*

at the same time."

— Thomas Merton

Water Lily No. 7

I couldn't take another second of her schoolmistress condescension. This time, I cut her off — not timidly, but with clarity.

"That was a joke," I said, the words firing from my mouth with unnerving precision. Our eyes locked — just for a moment — but it was enough. I knew then, with complete certainty, that we would not be friends in this lifetime.

And as for the image selection — it didn't go as smoothly as I'd hoped.
"To draw visitors to your stand, of course we'll need an eye-catcher," she began. "The piece I consider most suitable — based on size alone — is *Water Lily No. 7*."
She tapped a key. The painting appeared on the screen.

For one golden moment, all tension lifted. The noise in my head fell away. I wasn't in a sterile conference room anymore. I was drifting through a French landscape garden.
If, in that instant, a butterfly had risen from the canvas, slipped off the screen, and fluttered between us — I would have believed it.

I would have let the enchantment take me. I would have become an Impressionist. Time thinned to a trickle — not gone, exactly, but slowed to a shimmering pause.

But reality came crashing back with four clipped words: "That won't be possible."

"What?" she snapped — dry, sharp, as if her voice had blown in from the Sahara.

"That painting isn't mine anymore," I said. "I sold it recently."

"But your agency informed us that it would be available for the exhibition —"

"Maybe I hadn't yet reported the sale," I interrupted. "But the fact is: it's sold."
I stressed the last words — not angrily, but to end the matter.

Her posture shifted. Her eyes narrowed. She leaned toward me ever so slightly — a subtle but unmistakable shift in dynamic.
This painting, I now realized, was the cornerstone of my application.

Fragment. Studio wall, Frankfurt.

And then — just when I expected push-back — she surprised me. "Then get it back."

"What?" I stared, stunned.

"Borrow it from the buyer. Just for the duration of the exhibition."

I was speechless. "How... how do you imagine I do that? What am I supposed to say?"

She didn't blink."Tell him a painting only becomes a true artwork when it's been presented by a thoughtful artist to an appreciative audience. That's what you'll be giving him now — with your presentation at the Art-Fair."

Then, with the measured charm of someone well-versed in transactional elegance, she added:
"Give him concert tickets as a thank-you. Or offer him an extra piece from your portfolio. But get the painting back."

"Compromise,

if not the spice of life,

Is its solidity."

— Phyllis McGinley

The Price of Hanging

"It has to be worth it to you, Ms. Schneidermann," she said coolly. "But do make sure — under no circumstances — that the buyer is present at the official opening. If he starts talking in front of guests... well, you understand what I mean."

"But... I can't sell the same painting twice," I said, almost instinctively.

She looked at me like I was a dim child in Year Three, hovering just above failure.

"No, of course not," she replied, slowly, as if explaining subtraction. "We'll put a sticker on it from the start — *Reserved* or *Sold*. We'll handle that. But you must deliver the painting. Otherwise, I can't guarantee your participation in this year's exhibition."

Her gaze clung to me like static. There was no bluff in her voice. She meant it — absolutely.

I avoided looking out the window. My stomach tightened. Blood surged to my head. A strange, low buzzing began in my ears — a hint of tinnitus morphing into a high whine, rising in volume, in pressure.

"Ms. Schneidermann? Are you all right?" Her hand landed lightly on my shoulder.

And suddenly, like a cold snap across the face, the name returned:

Momberger. The buyer.

A stubborn conspiracy theorist with the aesthetic sense of a bulldozer. Art meant nothing to him — painting, even less. I once heard him suggest that Impressionists were a religious sect from North Africa.

He'd bought the painting for his wife, who adored it. At the time, I'd had the distinct feeling he was trying to make up for something — a betrayal, perhaps.

I strained to recall her face, but came up empty. Not a single feature surfaced. Strange.

But the very thought of contacting Momberger again — speaking to him, negotiating with him, *asking* him for something — made me nauseous.

The buzzing grew louder. The room tilted.

"This won't work," I said flatly, reaching for my water glass. I took a sip, shook my head.

"Ms. Schneidermann..." she said, almost gently, "I would truly regret having to strike you from the list here and now."

That was it. She wouldn't argue. She wouldn't bend. And I understood, with perfect clarity, that if I challenged her terms — if I so much as *questioned* them — I was out. Irrevocably out.

I was being swept along now, whether I agreed or not. And the truth was, I no longer had the energy to fight.

"There are still a few more things we need to go over," she added, shifting seamlessly back into protocol. "Topics such as dress code, etiquette — and a few helpful tips. After all, this is your first exhibition at this level, and we all want it to be a success. For all of us."

"Style is a simple way

of saying complicated things."

— Jean Cocteau

Between Art and Appearance

At the very least, I wanted to discuss these final points with her as an equal.

"Since this isn't an opera or a theatre gala," I began cautiously, "I assume I'm free, as an artist, to choose my outfit however I like — right?"

"Ms. Schneidermann," she replied, almost gently, "please don't be tempted to turn yourself into a work of art. Remember: your paintings are meant to be the focus — not you. The space will already be filled with sensory impressions. That's why, when it comes to your appearance, *less is more.*"

She continued in the same crisp, instructive tone: "Shorts or flip-flops are absolutely out of place at the opening. But arriving in a full evening gown would be overdressed. Aim for the middle. Think casual chic — timeless basics elevated by subtle style. I'd recommend a midi skirt with an over-sized sweater. And if your partner or husband is attending, he'll be just fine in a shirt and trousers with a relaxed cardigan."

"And what," I asked, drained but curious, "does your etiquette manual say about behavior?"

She had an answer ready. Of course.

"Refrain from loud commentary about the competition," she said crisply. "And avoid drawing attention to yourself by laughing at or disparaging any other artwork."

Then, surprisingly, her tone shifted — lighter, almost amused. "And don't worry if guests spend only a moment looking at your paintings. At the Metropolitan Museum in New York, the average visitor spends just thirty-two seconds per piece. So if someone barely glances at your work at the Art-Fair, they're probably just there for the free drinks."

Was the frost between us beginning to thaw?

I offered a tentative summary, testing the waters of reconciliation: "I understand — at any exhibition, there will be works you connect with, and others that leave you cold. Some people will find certain pieces beautiful. Others might dismiss them as dull, kitschy, or even irritating."

"That's exactly right," she said. "What we consider beautiful — or not — is often subjective. And that raises questions about the nature of perception itself."

I didn't quite follow, so I stayed silent.

That seemed to encourage her.

"Depending on your point of view, the beautiful can appear ugly, and the ugly beautiful. The philosopher Socrates spoke about the difference between appearance and essence — how something can be objectively beautiful, even if it isn't *perceived* as such. He said beauty is not what most people believe it to be. And he was right."

That she had retained such a thoughtful, philosophical view of art — in a business as cold and transactional as this — caught me off guard.

Her words stayed with me, long after the meeting had ended. There was a faint tightening in my throat — not unpleasant, just unexpected.

"We all carry within us
places of exile,

our crimes,
our ravages."

— Albert Camus

No Exit at Level Zero

Twenty-four hours to think it over — that was all she allowed me.

The shared costs — hall rental, display setup and takedown, guest catering, cleaning, advertising — totaled €3,800. Delivery, pickup, and shipping to buyers would be entirely my responsibility.

Art-Fair would take a commission on every sale. If the agreed-upon works — including *Water Lily No. 7* — weren't delivered on time, the organizers reserved the right to lease the space to a third party at short notice. Any resulting costs? Mine to cover.

Forty-five minutes later, I was back in the elevator. Someone had already pressed LEVEL 0 — *Exit.* I was alone as the cabin began its slow descent. I wasn't entirely sure I was awake — the hum of the cabin felt too even, too rehearsed, like the looped ambiance of a dream I didn't remember entering.

A curious sensation came over me — as though I were seated beside a broad, churning river. Turbid waters surged with relentless force, muffled and steady, carving their way through some unseen mountain gorge. A soft murmuring — like woven cloth dragged across stone — overlay the ambient sound. Here and there, driftwood bobbed to the surface, and in the foam, I imagined picture frames caught in eddies, being pulled under by invisible whirlpools.

A daydream crept in. It wanted to stay.

The elevator slowed. The doors opened. A woman entered.

Elegantly dressed. Mid to late thirties. She pressed a series of buttons in quick succession — not just selecting a floor, but as if trying to *seal herself in.*

Level 12. Level 11... No stops.

Level 0. Parking 1. Parking 2... We had reached the bottom — the *very* bottom.

The doors opened. She bolted, vanishing into the shadows between concrete pillars.

Lights flicked on, one by one, each with a fractional delay, casting an antiseptic glow. Her footsteps echoed, lingering. Cold, damp air drifted into the cabin.

Somewhere in the distance: a door slammed. An engine ignited. Tires screeched.

I pressed *Level 0 – Exit* — again, and again. Nothing.

I was alone. Stranded on a level I never meant to reach.

No signal on my phone.

Level 0. Parking. Somewhere else entirely.

In moments like these, you do what you must. I pressed the emergency button.

A brief delay. Then a voice — male, neutral. Familiar.

"Do you require assistance? Are you in danger? The stairwell is illuminated. You'll find it just to the left of the elevator. It leads directly to the Landgraf-Hermann-Straße exit."

The stairwell door resisted. When it finally gave way, a feral smell met me — the stale scent of a long-abandoned predator's cage.

The exit sign above flickered erratically, as though it too sensed something ending.

*"There are places in the heart
that do not yet exist;*

*suffering has to enter in for them
to come to be."*

— Léon Bloy

Chandeliers and Contracts

Martin had suggested Café Wiener for our meeting. Alongside its signature coffee specialties, it was said to serve the best *Taunus Torte* in Frankfurt. Tucked away on a quiet side street, the café was easily walkable from the Main Tower.

Martin and I had been close friends for years. He had studied art for a few semesters and was eager to hear about my appointment at Art-Fair — especially since I'd already described the lead-up to him in painstaking detail. His brief lunch break offered the perfect window. Besides, he was the only one with a Ford Transit big enough to transport my paintings.

The Wiener's interior exuded a gentle, worn elegance. The parquet floor creaked with every step; the marble tabletops were cool and smooth beneath my fingers. Wall mirrors and chandeliers conjured the spirit of Art Nouveau and Art Deco — the golden eras of European coffeehouse culture.

Waist-high wood paneling lent a sense of intimacy. Mirror tiles of varying lengths expanded the illusion of space. Sofa alcoves added velvety charm, and the entire café radiated the authentically worn character of the 1950s.

With practiced ease, I found a free table toward the back, pulled a Thonet chair closer, and sat.

It took me longer than it should have to remember how to summon a waiter in a traditional Viennese café: *"Herr Ober!"* But when I did, it worked like magic.

He appeared immediately — impeccably dressed, bow-tie knotted just so — unlike any server you'd find in a modern café.

"Bitt' schön – gnädigste," he said in the thickest Viennese dialect. I couldn't tell whether it was authentic or rehearsed — but it fit the setting, and that was what mattered.

"Just a regular coffee and your signature cream cake - the Taunus Torte," I said.

He stared blankly.

"There is no *regular* coffee here. Nor a latte macchiato. Nor an Americano," he replied dryly. "And the cream cake is out."

I asked what he *would* recommend. The gruffness softened. I ordered a Melange and a glass of water, knowing that from here I could read a newspaper for hours — or talk with Martin, even if he only had thirty minutes.

Of course, everything in me resisted the idea of sullying such a perfect atmosphere — this beautiful time capsule — with something as banal as contract clauses, shared costs, and delivery deadlines.

Still, I reached into my handbag and pulled out the folder.

As if to delay the inevitable, I let my gaze drift upward to study the chandeliers — when suddenly, a man appeared at my table.

"The beggar is not always the one who asks."

— Indian proverb

The Dog, the Deal, and the Drifter

At first, I thought it was Martin — but then I realized the man standing at my table was a drifter, trying to sell a homeless newspaper.

From beneath his stained summer coat peeked a red plaid flannel shirt. His thin, trembling legs were swallowed by tattered jeans, and the dust-covered leather boots he wore looked like they'd walked straight off the set of *The Tramp*. In one hand, he held a dog leash. At the end of it, a Jack Russell mix nosed around under the neighboring table, tending to the remains of someone's forgotten breakfast.

"Buy... would you buy the paper?" he stammered, lifting a copy of the *Workers' Gazette* as greasy strands of hair danced around his bristly beard.

For a moment, I was too startled to respond. Then I found myself wondering how he'd even gotten in here. I shook my head — firmly, deliberately.

"No," I said.

With emphasis, I turned back to the contract and took a sip of coffee. The Jack Russell sat, quiet and expectant. My rejection hadn't landed. The drifter was still there, unmoved.

"What do you want?" I barked.

"It's... it's for a good cause," he mumbled.

"Didn't you hear me? I said NO. Now get out of here!"

Loud enough for other tables to take notice.

His eyes glazed. I caught a flicker — something too brief to name. His shoulders slumped; the newspaper drooped in his hands as if gravity had turned mean. He turned and shuffled away, followed closely by what was likely his one and only friend in the world.

I watched them go, partly because I couldn't yet face the contract. Just before they reached the door, he turned and looked back — a hollow glance, unreachable.

Thank God, Martin arrived just then. He saved me from dwelling on it any longer. I quickly ordered two Melange and launched into a detailed account of my meeting with Art-Fair.

He listened carefully, visibly surprised by the terms and the costs — but didn't criticize. He knew this was the realization of a long-cherished dream.

"It's a big chance, no doubt about it. But you know every opportunity carries the possibility of failure. You're taking a considerable risk — financially, and artistically."

"Artistically?" I asked, caught off guard.

"Well, just look at the latest reviews of Art-Fair," he said. "The critics have been brutal. They say the artists have run out of ideas. *'Everything's already been done,'* they said."

"If art is to nourish the roots of our culture,

society must set the artist free."

— John F. Kennedy

Art, Comfort, and Contradictions

"But the events were always well attended," I countered.

"Yes, attended — sure. But do those visitors actually buy? Real buyers, the ones with real money — they don't want quaint, bourgeois pleasures. They want provocative objects. Art that confronts. Art shouldn't be *pleasing*."

Before I could respond, he added: "These days, art's viewed more and more as an investment anyway."

I was taken aback.

"But even Matisse said a good painting is like a good armchair. What's wrong with creating a space of aesthetic intimacy — where you connect with a beautiful picture in your own living room?"

I emphasized *beautiful* more than necessary.

Martin let out a short laugh and leaned back.

"Matisse was an Expressionist. He probably said that with irony — back in the early 20th century. More likely, he meant those paintings were *too* comfortable. Almost soporific. He and his contemporaries knew early on: connection doesn't come from harmony. It comes from tension — from discomfort."

Sensing I was on the defensive, I retreated.

"But a beautiful picture — that's harmony. That's perfection."

"Sorry," Martin said. "I see it differently. Art should build an expectation — and then *resist* it. The joy comes from puzzling, questioning, throwing out ideas and starting again. Without that? The joy thins fast. Too much of the same thing dulls the senses. Overexposure leads to fatigue."

I didn't know what to say.

"But *they want me*," I said, playing my ace. "Art-Fair and the bank want me."

As if that silenced critique.

"The bank wants to pose as a patron of the arts," he said. "Nice, tidy art for nice, tidy living rooms. And Art-Fair? They fill the booths. They make sure the sponsors don't walk away angry."

"The bank actually *buys* works from the exhibition. They're not doing that out of pity!"

"Sure," he shrugged. "Then they hang those pictures in their branches. Or above the buffet line in the canteen. Once a year, employees bid on them during the charity auction — and the proceeds go to the local kindergarten."

*"Art is not a mirror
held up to reality,*

*but a hammer
with which to shape it."*

— Bertolt Brecht

The Art of Self-Reflection

"Then there's room for new images, and the cycle begins again," I added, dryly.

Martin nodded. A pause lingered.

"Think about the kind of visitors you want to attract — and what *you* expect from art. I still remember your early work. It didn't fit any mold. There was upheaval. Curiosity. Boldness. You were searching for something new. And now? You've perfected Impressionism. Was that your gallery's suggestion?"

I began to reflect.

Yes, the art world was dynamic — full of possibilities. But it came with pitfalls. It allowed me to share my work widely, to connect. But it also posed risks: of compromise. Of dilution.

Commercialization was the core issue. Selling meant following trends — and that meant distancing myself from what mattered most.

The danger was subtle: I'd stop painting what I felt. I'd start painting what *sold*. And that road only led away from my artistic identity.

Exhibitors, galleries, agents — they offered access. But also, constraint. They favored what the market liked.

Experimental work? Often ignored.

Martin pointed out another layer:

"Digitalization. Social media. Sure, it opens up global reach. But it also pressures you to always *be visible.* And that push for visibility? It can twist your work toward what's viral — not what's authentic."

It hit me, then — painfully but clearly: I needed a conscious approach. One that aligned with *my* goals, not market metrics. Art that didn't just meet expectations — but served my own creative growth.

"Paint what you feel!" Martin said finally. Good friends, I was reminded, sometimes speak truths you don't want to hear.

His farewell was brief, warm, and left me with the bitter aftertaste of truth — and too much Melange.

"I am seeking. I am striving.

I am in it with all my heart."

— Vincent van Gogh

Paint What You Feel — Not What You See

I stepped out of the café with a strange sense of despair.

The world outside had shifted.
Somber.
Oppressive.
Faces of passersby distorted.
Loneliness and alienation crept over me like fog.

At the same time, something fierce stirred inside me — an urgent, unfamiliar compulsion. A need to express my inner sensations — raw, unfiltered.

Color exploded.
Contours hardened.
Perspective fractured.
Buildings leaned and twisted.
Gables bored into one another.
Windows bent.
Shadows stretched in impossible directions.

The world no longer obeyed natural laws. Only the café facade kept me grounded. Without it, I might have collapsed.

After the café. Everything changed.

My thoughts ignored logic — fragmented, erratic. And yet, a new rhythm took shape: one that mirrored the city's dissonance.

On the riverbank, plane trees glowed a violent blue. A woman with yellow skin, a green nose, and magenta hair walked *backward* across the Iron Bridge.
Outside the Cinema Museum, posters for *The Cabinet of Dr. Caligari* unfurled into infinity.

Then, **impact.**
Warmth.
Liquid.
Smell.
Coffee.
A splash across my chest. Stains spreading like continents on a pale blouse.
An empty to-go cup spun between my feet.
Children's laughter stopped.

A man ran across the street,
coat flapping like a flag.
A newspaper stuck from his pocket.
A small dog barked behind him.

Ernst Toller's *The Transformation* from 1919 came to mind. And I *felt* it — finally understood:

They light fires across the river.
Mysteries reveal themselves.

Outcast, I stumble
from one shore to the other.

A stranger to those over there,
alien to the others.

Grotesque hybrid.

"Alongside drugs and prostitution,

the art trade is the largest

unregulated market in the world."

— Georgina Adam,
Art Market Expert

Epilogue: The Art Market

Few markets are as defined by inequality as the art market. A handful of "painter princes" earn millions for their works, while 95% of artists cannot make a living from their art. According to the Art Market Report, the global art market generated around 65 billion USD in revenue in 2023.

Yet both nationally and internationally, the market is flooded with art. The quality of a work of art is inherently difficult to define. As a result, potential buyers face a problem of *fundamental uncertainty*.

Unlike other goods, art has no "functional value" that translates into practical utility. Nor can its value be determined by production costs.

The romantic notion of the lone genius creating singular masterpieces has long been divorced from reality.

To elevate an object to the status of "art," it also requires art critics, historians, curators, and gallerists to validate and contextualize it. A piece becomes art not by its material properties, but by the attributes assigned to it by actors in the art world.

Value. Constructed. Negotiated. Framed.

An object becomes art only when artists, critics, curators, gallerists, museum directors, and collectors collectively *agree* to treat it as such — regardless of whether, as the Munich art historian Piroschka Dossi ironically notes in her book *Hype. Art and Money*, it's an animal carcass, a nose job, or a pink poodle painted in acrylic.

The foundation for determining a work's economic value lies in the judgment of its aesthetic worth. That value, therefore, is a construction—and within that construction lies a certain arbitrariness.

It's important to understand that major galleries—such as Hauser & Wirth, Gagosian, David Zwirner, Pace, and White Cube — cooperate on an international scale. The artists they "discover," still largely unknown, are presented and marketed across continents in influential art hubs like New York, London, and Hong Kong.

The art market, in turn, tends to privilege Western concepts of art, while other artistic traditions and forms of expression remain underrepresented.

This shift has also transformed the very nature of art. Depth, ambiguity, and risk are increasingly unwelcome. Art is increasingly shaped by a superficial consumer aesthetic.

Ulli Seegers, in his book *Ethics in the Art Market*, puts it this way:

"It's about a kind of aesthetic that's no longer risky, but reflects our current times and is therefore socially acceptable. I'm not suggesting that art with long-term historical significance no longer exists today, but the pursuit of new 'isms,' styles, or com-pelling artistic positions that may remain histori-cally relevant for the next hundred years—that pur-suit has largely given way to viewing art as an in-vestment."

Perhaps the greatest illusion of
all

is not what art reveals

—

but who gets to decide
it matters.

Author and Licensing

Wolfgang Steih, studied computer science and started his career as a programmer. Until 2017, he worked as a solution architect in the business development department of an international corporation when the opportunity arose. Disillusioned by his stressful job, he seized the opportunity and left his career to devote himself to self-reflection, writing, and abstract painting. Today, he lives near Frankfurt and complements his activities with a degree in philosophy. *The Painter on Floor Thirty-Six* is his debut novel in English.